SIÔN and the BARGAIN BEE

Jenny Sullivan

Jac Jones

First Impression — 1998

ISBN 1 85902 621 4

To Landsdowne Primary School,
A Happy Hundredth Birthday

This book is Published with the support
of the Arts Council of Wales

Printed in Wales
at Gomer Press, Llandysul, Ceredigion

No one could call Siôn idle. Except his Mam, who called him 'idle' about twice a day. The rest of the time she called him 'lazy', 'indolent', and 'useless', sometimes all together in the same sentence. She usually finished with 'What did I do to deserve a son like you?', but Siôn loved her anyway.

He'd once had a job guarding a farmer's prize pig, but pigs like to sleep a lot, to help them grow fat. Siôn's snoring was so loud it had kept the pig awake, and it became as thin as a pin and died. Then Siôn had no job at all, and soon the day came when there was no money to pay the rent. Their cows had to go.

'Sell them, Siôn,' his Mam said. 'Make sure you get plenty of gold. Goodness knows, we need every penny.'

So Siôn set off with cows Rhiannon, Branwen and Gwenhwyfar. Half-way to the market, he met a little man.

'*Bore da*,' Siôn said, for even if he was idle, he was always polite.

'And good morning to you, my fine lad. And where are you away this glorious day?' The man had blue, twinkly eyes, and Siôn liked him at once.

'I'm taking our cows to market.' Siôn scratched Branwen behind her horn. 'I'm supposed to sell them for a lot of gold. Don't want to, mind,' he added. 'I like a drop of fresh milk of a morning. Besides, these cows are like old friends. It don't feel right to be selling them.'

'Then don't,' the little man said, spreading his unusually large hands. 'Give them to me, instead. They will have a fine life with me. In return, I will give you this amazing club, this wonderful music box and this beautiful bee in a fine glass bottle.'

Siôn frowned. 'But I need money to pay the rent, not old clubs and stuff.'

The little man winked a merry eye. 'These are worth much more than gold.'

'Are you sure?' Siôn may have been cabbage-looking, but he certainly wasn't green. 'There was a bloke who got a beanstalk with a giant on it. I don't like giants.'

'No one with brains would swap a cow for beans,' the little man replied. 'But an intelligent lad would swap his cows for these.'

A man with hands as large as those, Siôn thought, must surely be kind and generous. He decided in an instant. 'Done and dusted!' He took the club, the bottle and the music box, and gently patted the cows goodbye.

Trouble was, the closer he got to home, the less pleased Siôn felt Mam was going to be with his bargains.

Mam was washing the kitchen floor. 'Well?' she demanded, 'where's the gold?'

'Um.' Siôn shuffled his feet. 'I didn't get gold. I got these, instead.' And he showed his Mam the club, the bee and the music box.

'Aaargh!' Siôn's Mam upended the bucket of dirty water over his head. 'You half-baked dolt, you nincompoop, you stupid booby, you *twpsyn*, you, you — shufflenoddle!'

She'd never called him that before. She wailed. She wept. She howled. She bellowed.

'Oh, my lovely cows,' she cried, 'gone, and all for this *rubbish!*'

Siôn cautiously lifted the bucket and peered out. His Mam looked horribly cross. The dog was hiding under the table, and the cat was cowering well out of Mam's reach. Siôn wished he could hide too.

'Oh me, oh my,' she wailed. 'When the Squire comes on Monday, that'll be it. Out we shall be, lock, stock and barrel, sure as eggs is eggs and apples is apples. And it's all your fault, Siôn!'

Mam rolled up her sleeves and glared at Siôn. Her look promised a very sore sit-upon. Quickly, Siôn snatched up the music box and turned the handle.

At the first tinkly notes, Mam was transformed. First her left foot twitched, then her right foot tapped. She lifted her skirt to her knees, stuck out her elbows and began to dance.

She tripped. She twirled. She tromped. She tiptoed.

She tangoed and she terpsicated.

She swooped, she soared, she swayed, she swung.

Siôn turned the handle faster. Mam's shoes were smouldering, the soles almost worn out.

'Oh, stop, stop!' she sobbed.

'Promise you won't beat me?' Siôn kept turning the handle and his Mam danced on and on.

'Oh, I promise, I promise.'

So Siôn stopped.

And Mam collapsed in a heap.

Someone hammered on the door.

'Where's my rent?' demanded the Squire.

'Haven't got it,' Siôn blurted. His Mam poked him to shut up.

'Oh, Sir, Sir, I'm just a poor old woman, with —'

But the Squire wasn't listening. 'No money, no cottage,' he said angrily. 'Out, the pair of you.'

'But we've nowhere else to go,' Mam pleaded.

'Then sleep in a hedge!' roared the Squire, his face red with fury.

As if in answer to the Squire's bellowing, the club, which leant against the wall by the washtub, twitched. The Squire took no notice. The club twitched again, rose in the air, and moved slowly towards him. *Then* he noticed!

'Wh-wh-what's *that?*' he gasped.

'You'll find out,' Siôn said. He wasn't sure what would happen, but he knew that something would.

It did. The club floated across to the Squire, and began to beat him without mercy.

'Ow! said the Squire, and ran. 'Getitoffme! I'll have the constable on — Ouch! Ooch!'
The club chased the Squire as he fled down the path.

Whap!

Whop!

Whomp!

Whump!

Then it whapped him, whopped him, whomped him and whumped him all over again.
The Squire ran as fast as his fat legs would carry him, over the hill and far away.

'That club's better than a big dog!' Mam said. 'Doesn't leave blood on my nice clean floor, neither.' Then she frowned. 'But he'll be back, I 'spect.'

So Siôn had been rescued twice by his bargains. First the music box, and then the club. Now he wondered what magical powers the bee in the bottle had. He held it up to the light and examined it. It was a very fine bee, and no mistake. But what was it *for*?

He decided all at once that he should go and seek his fortune, rather than wait for the Squire to come back and his Mother to lose her temper again. So he packed up some bread and cheese, a clean hanky, the club and the bee in the bottle and kissed his Mam goodbye.

'I'll leave you the music box in case the Squire pesters you again, Mam,' he said. 'I won't come back until I've found my fortune.'

'Fat chance!' his Mam said. But she kissed him goodbye and even sniffled a little.

Siôn walked and walked, and just as the sun was slipping behind the mountains and his feet were getting sore he came to a fine, big house next to a ruined castle.

Siôn went to the back door of the house and knocked. Two ladies as alike as two Caerffili cheeses (and about as round) opened the door. Siôn asked politely if he could rest there overnight. The servants, Phyllis and Dilys, were pleased to have a young visitor and invited him in.

'Come in, sit down, have a nice cup of tea –' said Phyllis.

'–and a Welshcake?' Dilys offered the plate.

Siôn didn't need inviting twice. He had some chicken and an apple, too.

'Pity about that castle falling down,' he said (but not with his mouth full).

'Falling down?' said Phyllis, 'oh, it en't fallin' down, young feller. Hit's bein' builded *hup!* On'y as fast as His Lordship builds it, something comes along at night and knocks it down again!' She passed Siôn a biscuit. 'And His Lordship said, on'y last night he said, didn't he, Dilys? He said, "If someone could find out who's doing it," he said, "why, he could marry Seren, my daughter!"'

'Did he, now?' Siôn was interested. 'Is Seren pretty?'

Dilys cackled. 'Pretty? She's pretty enough to make birds fall out of trees, she is!'

Siôn resolved to stay up all night and find out who or what was knocking down His Lordship's castle.

Staying awake all night is difficult, and Siôn kept dropping off and waking up, dropping off and waking up. Then, suddenly, he was WIDE awake. He heard a strange noise.

Thuddddd, thuddddd, thuddddd, thuddddd.

And there, thumping up the hill, were two enormous, ugly giants. They were very hairy, and very bare. They stepped across the castle wall and at once began to demolish the castle.

‘That’s vandalism, that is,’ Siôn thought. ‘That’s disgraceful!’ And he was so cross that without thinking (he was good at not thinking!) he picked up a stone and chucked it at the giants. It bounced off the bare, warty head of the uglier one.

‘A-a-a-aw!’ it said. ‘Woffore did you do that, our Ogwen?’

‘Didn’t.’

‘Did!’

‘Didn’t.’ And Ogwen turned his back on the bald one and got on with demolishing the wall.

Siôn threw another stone. It hit the other giant.

'Ouch!' He rubbed his ear. 'You playin' silly beggars, our Maldwyn? You pelted a stone at me, you did. My ear is all a-hurtin'.'

'Tweren't me.'

'Twere!'

'Tweren't!'

Maldwyn poked Ogwen in the nose, hard. Ogwen punched Maldwyn. Maldwyn clouted Ogwen, harder.

The two giants hurled themselves into a tangled, shoving, kicking mass, pulling hair, walloping noses and crunching heads. Siôn sat up high on the wall and watched. It was very noisy.

They fought until the moon was going down and the sun was coming up. Even the bats were going home to bed. And then, suddenly, they stopped.

It was very quiet. Both giants were very still. Not even a toenail twitched. Slowly, carefully, ready to run if need be, Siôn crept down from his perch. The giants were exceedingly quiet. Incredibly still. Undoubtedly — dead!

They had each beaten the other as dead as a doornail.

'Hooray — now to claim my reward!' said Siôn.

Siôn washed his face and hands in Phyllis's kitchen, Dilys combed his hair, and as soon as His Lordship was up and at his breakfast, Siôn told his tale.

'You may build your castle as high as you like,' Siôn began. 'I have killed both the giants who were knocking it down.' (That wasn't strictly true, of course, but it made a better story.)

'A shrimp like you killed two giants?' His Lordship said incredulously. 'What, *you?*'

'Me, my Lord,' Siôn said proudly. 'I, myself, personal-like. And I claim your daughter's hand in marriage.'

His Lordship tossed a bone to his hounds and they squabbled over it. Marry his daughter? A skinny, shabby, penniless *peasant?* That wouldn't do at all!

'Ah,' he said shiftily, wiping his mouth on a napkin. 'H'm. There's just one other thing, young fellermelad, before I hand over Seren, my beautiful daughter . . .'

I knew there'd be a catch, Siôn thought glumly. Always is, right?

He sighed. 'And what might that be, Sire?'

'Ah — there's this piggie in the forest. I need you to kill it. It's been a terrible nuisance. And if you can kill two giants, a little pig shouldn't give you much trouble, should it?'

Siôn was still suspicious, but he wasn't going to let on. 'No problem, Sire,' he said. 'Roast pork for supper!'

His Lordship hid a smile.

When Siôn told Phyllis and Dilys what His Lordship had said, they were indignant.

'There's a swizz!' Dilys said. 'He promised you could marry Seren if you sorted out whoever was breaking down his walls, and now he's making you go after the terrible, fierce, awful, wild boar!'

'Pardon?' Siôn was alarmed. 'Wild boar? What wild boar? Terrible? Fierce? He said it was a little piggie!'

'He would say that, wouldn't he?' Dilys muttered. 'Don't want you to marry his precious daughter, I'll be bound. Nasty old cheat!'

'Well, I can't get out of it now,' Siôn said glumly. 'I went and promised him, didn't I? Can I borrow a nice, strong rope, please?'

Phyllis found him the rope while Dilys made him a tasty packed lunch with Caerffili cheese, apples and *teisen lap*. They wept as they waved him goodbye, certain they'd never see him again.

Siôn walked into the deep, dark wood, the rope over one shoulder, his stick with his picnic on the end over the other. When he came to the biggest tree in the forest, he opened the cloth containing the food and spread it out on the ground, all except for one apple, which he ate himself, because he was a growing lad. Then he climbed up the tree, tied the rope round the strongest branch he could find and waited.

A whole hour passed. Two hours. Three.

Then the wild boar arrived.

It was the ugliest creature Siôn had ever seen, with piggy red eyes and monstrous tusks. It fell upon Siôn's picnic and chomped up the cheese, the apples and the pies. While it was eating, Siôn threw down the rope, deftly lassoed the boar and hauled the rope tight.

The boar heaved and fought and butted the tree-trunk, almost shaking Siôn off his perch! But eventually, its hairy body lay still. It was quite dead, strangled by the rope.

Siôn told His Lordship the job was done.

'You killed that monstrous boar?' His Lordship gasped.

'It was just a little piggie, Sire!'

His Lordship sent men to find the boar and bring it back.

'And now, my Lord,' Siôn said, prodding the boar's rump with his foot, 'may I meet my future wife?'

'Who?' His Lordship asked.

'Why, Seren!' Siôn had a funny feeling His Lordship would try to cheat him. He was right, of course.

'What, you marry Seren?' His Lordship declared, 'Certainly not!'

'You promised me Seren, Seren I shall have!' Siôn said. He pulled out the bottle containing the bee.

He whipped off the top and the furious bee flew straight at His Lordship. It stung him on his bottom, it stung him on his ear, it stung him on his neck, both his legs and the end of his nose.

'All right, all right, you can marry her!' he shrieked. 'Mercy, mercy, mercy!'

'You're quite sure?' Siôn asked sternly. 'Only I don't want you going back on your promise again. That isn't honest, and a fine gentleman like you ought to be honest, you know.'

'I promise, I promise,' shrieked His Lordship.

'Right!' Siôn gave one shrill whistle, the bee flew obediently back into the bottle and His Lordship collapsed in a heap on the floor, moaning loudly.

Siôn and Seren fell in love just as they should. She was (naturally) beautiful, and she thought Siôn was kind and handsome as well as brave. They married at once, though not before Siôn had taken Seren to visit his mother, who of course had been without any money while Siôn was seeking his fortune. She was down to her very last crust, so Siôn returned just in time, before she starved to death.

For her wedding, Seren wore a beautiful white silk dress with bows and flounces, and carried a bouquet so large that it almost hid her entirely.

His Lordship gave Siôn a fine suit of blue cloth to wear, and was surprised to discover that, dressed in posh clothes, Siôn didn't look like a peasant after all. Well, not much, anyway. So His Lordship gave Seren away with good grace, and danced (with a bandage on his bee-stung nose) with Mam at the wedding feast. The strange little man with the generous hands and the blue, blue eyes came, too — even though no one remembered inviting him.

Afterwards, Siôn and Seren and Mam settled down in the new castle, and on dark winter evenings Mam would turn the handle of the music box and Siôn and Seren, his Star, would dance and dance.

But only until their shoes wore out!